Bad Habits: A MMF Romance

Isla Chiu

Published by Isla Chiu, 2021.

Table of Contents

Skinny-dipping leads to an encounter with a handsome duke

Under the moonlight, Persephone Danbury gasped when her friend Mary slipped out of her habit.

"Why are you gasping, dear Persephone?" Mary asked with a laugh. "You're acting as if you've never seen naked breasts before."

Persephone's fair cheeks turned pink as she avoided looking at Mary's bare bosom. "I thought we were going swimming."

"And we are," Mary said, taking a few steps toward Persephone. Persephone's blush deepened. How did Mary walk around in her naked form with such confidence and not a hint of embarrassment? Persephone felt like dying of mortification whenever someone gazed upon her *bare ankle*. "Do you think we could go swimming in these heavy habits? We would drown."

Persephone's pulse raced as Mary played with her collar. "You could've kept your undergarments on."

Mary shrugged, her red waves of hair swaying in the breeze. Persephone's eyes couldn't help wandering toward her friend's hair. Her father, the Viscount of Leister, frequently claimed that people with red hair were absolutely vile and hideous, but Persephone often found herself enchanted by Mary's beautiful hair and bright green eyes. "How would we explain wet undergarments to the nuns?"

Her friend had a point. The nuns at St. Camilla's Convent weren't unkind, but they frowned upon frivolity and would certainly consider swimming in one's undergarments to be an act of frivolity. "Honestly, the things that you persuade me to do," Persephone muttered. She started taking off her clothes until she noticed that Mary was staring at her unabashedly. "Um, may I have a moment of privacy?"

"All right," Mary said. She waved at Persephone as she ran toward the lake. "I'll see you in the water later."

Persephone shook her head, but a smile tugged at her lips. Her father definitely would have disapproved of Mary. The viscount thought that the ideal young woman was modest and quiet. Mary, however, was confident and outspoken. But Persephone liked Mary precisely for the reasons why her father wouldn't have.

When the viscount had told Persephone that he was sending her to a convent, she had been hurt and afraid. She knew that her father had done so because he thought her to be one of the greatest disappointments of his life. Before she'd been born, her mother had suffered multiple miscarriages because the viscount had been determined to have a son. Eventually, her mother had given birth to a child, but it had resulted in her death. Worse, the child was only a useless girl.

Her father's disappointment had only grown as Persephone grew older. By all accounts, she was a stunning raven-haired beauty, but no one was willing to marry her because of how small her dowry was. Although her father was a viscount, he couldn't afford to give her a large dowry because he sunk most of his money into gambling and prostitutes.

After she had endured four seasons in London without getting a single proposal, the viscount had decided that he'd had enough of her worthless presence. Thus, he'd sent her away to St. Camilla's Convent.

To Persephone's surprise, life at the convent wasn't miserable. She had envisioned cruel nuns with canes that they weren't afraid to use and use often, kneeling for hours on hard floors as they prayed to St. Camilla and God, and endless bowls of flavorless gruel.

But the nuns weren't cruel hags. Sure, they were strict and a tad dull, but they cared more about Persephone's well-being than her own father ever did. And though they prayed a lot, they didn't have to kneel for hours on uncomfortable floors. And the food wasn't bad either. They often had fresh vegetables from the garden and sometimes had rabbits that the nuns caught with their traps.

Persephone shivered as she took off her habit. Why hadn't Mary suggested a swim on a warmer night? She looked around her, making sure no eyes watched her as she slipped out of her undergarments. Once she was naked, she let out a breath and hugged herself for warmth. Then she ran toward the lake.

"Why, Persephone, you have such lovely ankles," Mary teased, her eyes definitely *not* looking at Persephone's ankles.

Persephone felt the entirety of her body go red before lowering herself into the lake. She almost yelped; the water was colder than she expected. But after a few moments, she relaxed and found the water to be refreshing against her skin. She looked up at the dark sky. The full moon was so bright.

Mary played with a lock of Persephone's hair. Heat filled Persephone's body, heat that wasn't entirely due to embarrassment. Before she'd moved to the convent, she'd never imagined doing *things* with a woman — her intolerant father would've beaten her for such thoughts — but sometimes, when she was with Mary, she wondered...

"You really are a lovely thing," Mary murmured. "How did no man end up proposing to you?"

"A big dowry is worth more than a pretty face," Persephone said, trying to keep the bitterness out of her voice and succeeding only somewhat.

A corner of Mary's lips curved up. "Oh well, I doubt that any man is good enough for my Persephone anyway."

More heat filled Persephone at the words "*my* Persephone." Why did she enjoy Mary's use of a possessive pronoun so much?

Persephone jumped at the sound of rustling leaves. Oh no, what if it was one of the nuns? They would get in so much trouble...

A smile lit up Mary's face. "Hello, handsome."

Persephone felt her heart sink at the sight of James, Mary's current beau. Her heart sank further when James lowered his head to kiss Mary.

"Are you two girls naked?" James asked with a grin that prompted Persephone to cross her arms over her chest though the water hid her breasts from view.

Boldly, Mary climbed out of the lake, putting her nude body on display. "Does this answer your question?" she asked, wrapping her arms around James.

"My God, Mary," James said. "You could bring any man to his knees."

Mary asked in a low voice, stroking his cheek, "Am I going to see you on your knees tonight?"

"I do have my master's carriage..."

Mary turned to Persephone. "Will you be fine returning to the convent by yourself?"

Persephone forced herself to smile. "Yes, I'll be fine. Have a good night, Mary."

After Mary picked up her clothes and ran off with James, Persephone let out a sigh. Mary was always running around with boys (without the nuns' knowledge of course). She'd asked Persephone a couple of times if she would like to meet her beau's friends, but Persephone was always uneasy around members of the opposite sex, which was why she'd hated going to London for the season.

Persephone jumped again when she heard the sound of rustling leaves again. Was it Mary returning to her? She turned around, paling when she saw a smirking young man.

"Are my eyes deceiving me or do I see a naked maiden in front of me?" he asked.

Persephone's heart raced. She reached for her clothes, but the man spotted her movement and grabbed her clothes before she could.

Scoundrel, she thought, suppressing a scowl. She hugged herself, covering up her breasts. Oh, why had she agreed to go for a night swim?

"Do you want your clothes back?" he asked with undisguised glee.

Though she instantly hated the stranger, she couldn't help noting how handsome he was. Golden hair, bright hazel eyes, the facial structure of a Greek god. He wore fine, expensive clothes that marked him as a member of the nobility. He seemed familiar. Had she seen him at a ball last season?

Her face lost all remaining color as she realized his identity. He was Marcus Elham, the Duke of Charlotteshire. Unlike her father, he was extremely wealthy — and extremely powerful.

"Can you speak, fair maiden, or are you mute?" he asked.

She wished she could throw a stone at his head. "I can speak."

He smiled. "So fair maiden who can speak, do you or do you not want your clothes back?"

She clenched her teeth. "I do want my clothes back, so if you could hand them to me, I would be much obliged."

Ignoring her, he mused, "A habit. So you're from the convent…"

"Excellent deduction," she muttered.

"Was that a sarcastic remark? I thought that nuns weren't allowed to be sarcastic."

She wanted to snort. Some of the nuns at St. Camilla's Convent were definitely sarcastic, especially Sister Grace, who loved to give Persephone a hard time for her "extraordinarily poor arithmetic skills."

"May I have my clothes back?" she asked, near the edge of desperation.

"That depends…"

Frustration brewed in her. "Depends on what?"

He lowered his head, grabbing her chin. "If you're willing to give me a kiss."

Before she could push him away or slap him, he put his mouth on hers. She caught her breath. She had kissed a few boys before, but the kisses had always been chaste; they might as well have been pecks from her grandmother. This kiss from the duke, however, was anything but chaste. He thrust his tongue between her lips, threatening to completely consume her. And for some reason, she liked — no, *loved* — it.

He traced a pattern on her cheek. "You're a truly exquisite thing."

She glared at him. "May you leave now? I wish to have some privacy as I put my clothes back on."

"No," he said infuriatingly.

She loathed dukes and other rich noblemen. They acted as if they were entitled to anything and everything. Even some poor noblemen — like her own father — possessed this sense of entitlement.

A shiver climbed down her back. She did not want to climb out of the water and allow the Duke to see her nude. But she also did not wish to freeze to death.

Letting out a breath, she got out of the lake, covering her bosom and feminine flesh. Mortification threatened to set her body on fire as the Duke shamelessly stared at her.

"Exquisite," he said in a low voice.

"May you hand me my clothes?" she asked, wishing she could claw his eyes out.

With an exaggerated sigh, he handed her the bundle of clothing. She thought about asking him to turn around as she put her clothes back on, but he most likely would have refused her request, so she didn't waste her breath and got into her habit as fast as she could.

He held her chin. "You really are too pretty to be a nun."

"I need to — "

He pulled her to him, pressing his body against hers and leaving her breathless. His eyes burning into hers, he caressed her mouth.

She widened her eyes as she became aware of a new hardness against her thigh. *Oh my God,* she thought. She knew little about the relations between men and women, but she knew that the hardness was not due to wood in his pocket and that it would bring her absolutely no good.

So she kicked his shin, causing him to yelp and let go of her. Then she ran back to the convent as if her life depended on it.

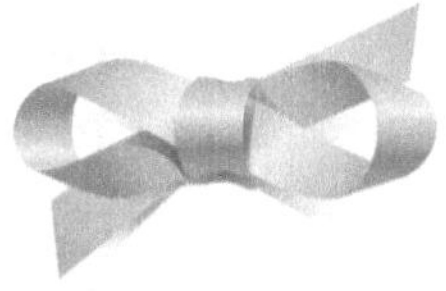

The duke makes a mess in his carriage

Marcus raised his eyebrow ever so slightly at James, his coachman. His shirt was rumpled. And... "You left the buttons on your trousers undone," he pointed out.

James looked down at himself and blanched. Rushing to fasten his buttons, he said, "Thank you, your grace. I apologize for my disheveled appearance. I was, um..."

A smirk came onto Marcus's mouth. "Were you having a rendezvous with a girl, James?"

His poor coachman stammered, "Your grace, I, um, I, uh..."

Marcus patted James's shoulder. "Relax. You're a red-blooded male. It would be foolish for me to not expect you to have any fun with women."

James bowed his head. "Thank you, your grace."

"No need to thank me," the duke said. "Now may you drive me home?"

"Of course, your — "

"James, you don't need to address me as 'your grace' in *every* sentence."

"If you say so, your, um..." The coachman blushed.

The duke smiled to himself as he climbed into the carriage. His coachman was adorable.

His smile faded as his shin throbbed. A curse escaped his lips when he rubbed it. For a petite thing, the beautiful nun had kicked him surprisingly hard. The staff of life between his thighs hardened as he recalled the sight of her naked curves. She really was an exquisite creature.

Intense need burned through his blood. He *had* to have her. He was fairly certain that seducing a nun was an outrageous sin, even by his standards. Oh well, it wasn't as if he was ever meant to go to heaven.

The nun hadn't seemed to particularly like him — his throbbing shin was painful proof of her dislike — but she had responded quite favorably to his stolen kiss. He would have bet his estate that she would respond *very* favorably to him stealing her innocence...

"James, may you drive me to St. Camilla's Convent tomorrow?"

"Of course, your...um, I mean..."

Marcus shot him a grin. "You may call me 'your grace' in every sentence if you cannot help it, James."

"Noted, your grace."

Exhaling, the duke leaned back against his seat. He couldn't wait for tomorrow. He closed his eyes, his cock aching as he thought of the gorgeous nun's long black curls, sparkling violet eyes, and plump bosom. God, he had so badly wanted to ravish her under the moonlight. He did not care what it took; he was going to find out who she was, and he was going to have her.

Not giving a damn if James saw — actually, the idea of James watching him made him more aroused — the duke tugged at his trousers, freeing his swollen manhood. He gripped his cock, moaning.

"Are you all right, your grace?" James asked in alarm.

"Thank you for your concern, but I'm quite all right," Marcus managed to say. "I'm just exercising some urgent needs as a red-blooded male."

"Oh, I see...um, noted, your grace."

Marcus hissed, running his hand up and down his erection. God, how he wished his cock was inside the nun's cunt now. He would have gambled with his life that it would feel like heaven, though it would be a soul-damning sin to seduce a young woman into breaking her vows with God.

With a cry, he came, coating the floor of the carriage with his cum.

His cry reached the ears of James, who sighed and thought, *I suppose I'm going to have to clean the coach tonight.*

The ribbon of desire

In the morning, Persephone went to the market to buy eggs and flour for the convent. As Sister Grace handed her some coins, she teased, "This is the exact change for the eggs and flour, Persephone. I'm not going to allow the grocer to take advantage of your poor arithmetic skills again."

Persephone reddened. The last time she'd gone to the grocer, he'd taken all of her coins and not given her any change. When Sister Grace had discovered this, she'd been furious.

"That skinflint didn't give you any change?" Sister Grace hissed.

"Was he supposed to?" Persephone asked innocently.

Sister Grace's eyes turned into slits. "Did you not add up the prices of the goods before purchasing them?"

Persephone stammered, her face hot with embarrassment, "Um, well..."

Sister Grace rolled her eyes and muttered, "Why do nobility insist on teaching their daughters how to hold their teacups in a charming manner instead of useful things like basic arithmetic?"

At those words, Persephone's blush darkened. Her father had insisted on teaching her how to sip tea in such a way that it would attract (ideally wealthy) suitors and told her that noblewomen had no need to "learn boring things like history, science, or mathematics." Before she'd begun donning a habit, she would go shopping with her maid, and her maid would always handle the money, so she truly had no need to even do basic addition in her head.

Fortunately, Sister Grace had marched over to the grocer, and after she'd given him a severe tongue-lashing, he'd handed the nun her change, plus an extra pound for the inconvenience he'd caused her.

Since then, Sister Grace would tease Persephone for her lack of mathematical skills.

Now, at the sight of Persephone's red face, Sister Grace smiled and patted her hot cheek affectionately. "You know I'm only having fun with you, dear."

"I know," Persephone said, relaxing. Mary disliked Sister Grace because she believed she was much too mean to Persephone, but Persephone knew that Sister Grace meant no malice and cared for her under her mocking words. Unlike Persephone's father, who possessed no affection under his cruel words.

Persephone bowed her head. "I'll return soon with the eggs and flour, Sister Grace."

"Take your time, Persephone."

Because of the nice weather, Persephone did take her time as she walked to the market. The sun was bright and warm, but not so warm that it made wearing her habit uncomfortable.

As she headed to the grocer's stand, her lips tingled as she remembered the duke's kiss last night. He had been an arrogant scoundrel, but she'd dreamed about his kiss, and the dreams had caused her to wake up with a new wetness in her undergarments.

She shivered as she recalled feeling his hardness. She was thankful that she'd been able to run away. Who knew what the duke would've done if she'd stayed? Arrogant noblemen like him frequently felt free to take liberties with unfortunate young women.

She stopped, getting the strange feeling that someone was watching her. Her mouth went dry with fear. Could it be the duke? Her eyes darted around the market before she locked eyes with a man in a black jacket.

The man continued staring at her without the least bit of embarrassment. She flushed. Like the duke, this man was also attractive. But whereas the duke looked like a Greek god, this man looked like he could be a brooding hero in one of Mary's romance novels. He was tall, dark, and handsome, and seemed equally likely to kiss you or strangle you.

She tore her gaze away from him and resumed her walk toward the grocer's stand. She needed to get eggs and flour, not waste her time wondering about strange — if handsome — men.

"Hello."

She nearly dropped her basket at the sound of the stranger's voice. How had he appeared by her side without her noticing? Was he a vampire or simply a very, very fast walker? She glanced at his long legs. Probably the latter, but she gripped the cross around her neck tightly just in case.

She bowed her head politely. "Hello." She took a closer look at the man's attire. It was elegant and fine, practically screaming wealth.

"Do you need help carrying your basket?"

She blinked, resisting the urge to reply, *Do I need help carrying my empty basket?* "No, but thank you for the offer."

His dark eyes gazed into hers. She turned pink, avoiding his stare. Had she unknowingly rubbed an oil that attracted strange handsome men on her body? First the duke, now this man.

"You're exceedingly lovely," he murmured. "A shame that you're a nun."

She bowed her head again, discomfort rolling around in her belly. "Um, thank you for your kind words. I must run some errands. So, um, have a good day, sir."

To her dismay, instead of leaving her be, he followed her to the grocer.

As Persephone approached the grocer, he swallowed, seeming nervous. He was probably remembering the last interaction he'd had with Sister Grace. "What would you like today, miss?" he asked.

"A dozen eggs and a bag of flour," she said. She started to lift the coins out of her purse, but before she could hand the money to the grocer, the handsome man/possible-vampire dropped some silver onto the grocer's palm.

"She'll also like a carton of strawberries and chocolate truffles," the stranger said.

"Wait, I don't — " she began to say.

"I insist," he said in a low voice, his lips only centimeters away from her ear.

The grocer shrugged. "The gentleman's money is as good as yours, miss." Before Persephone could protest, he placed the goods in her basket.

"But — " she said.

The handsome stranger whisked her away from the grocer before she could finish her sentence.

"I need to return the strawberries and chocolate," she said. When she tried to go back to the grocer, he wrapped an arm around her waist.

"Do you like ribbons?" he asked.

She blinked. Deciding to ignore his absurd question, she said, "I cannot accept these things from you. It'd be improper — "

"Who bloody cares about what's proper?"

She muttered, "You evidently do not."

A corner of his mouth tilted up. "Indeed, I do not. What is your name?"

"Athena," she lied.

He clicked his tongue. "You're trying to give me a false name, aren't you? I thought nuns weren't supposed to lie."

"I'm not lying." Of course, she blushed, giving away her dishonesty.

He clicked his tongue again. "No matter. I'll eventually find out your real name, *Athena*. I'm Thomas Ellison, and that is the truth."

The name sounded faintly familiar. Her eyes nearly leapt out of her head. Was he *the* Thomas Ellison, the tycoon who had lifted himself out of poverty and recently become one of the wealthiest men in England?

As if reading her mind, he said, "Yes, I am *that* Thomas Ellison."

She felt like running away, but he, seeming to read her mind again, tightened his hold on her.

He directed them to a vendor who offered a variety of fine silk ribbons. "Which one would you like?" he asked.

"I'm a nun," she said. "I have no use for ribbons." And even if she wasn't a nun, she would still be reluctant to accept a gift from a male stranger. The majority of men didn't give expensive presents out of the goodness of their hearts.

"I think red would suit you marvelously," he said. Then he asked the vendor, "May I have a red ribbon?"

The vendor said, "Of course, sir."

Persephone said, "I don't need — "

He actually had the audacity to put a finger to her lips and shush her. "You may not need it, but I'm sure you want it."

She scowled at him as he paid for the ribbon. She couldn't decide who was more irritating — the duke or Thomas.

He dragged her to a secluded spot by the woods at the edge of the market. "Let's sit," he said.

"I can't sit and get my habit dirty."

"Fair enough," he said, making her think that he would let her go. Instead, he sat on the ground and pulled her onto his lap.

Heat threatened to burn her face. "What are you doing? This isn't proper."

"You said you didn't want to get your habit dirty. And I told you, I do not give a damn about what's proper."

Before she could protest, he removed her wimple.

"Such a shame you must cover up this beautiful hair," he murmured, playing with one of her black curls.

She tried to grab her wimple from his hand, but he stuffed it inside his jacket before she could get ahold of it. "Please give my wimple back to me," she said through clenched teeth.

"Later."

He touched her neck, causing her to quiver in something not unlike pleasure. Then he pulled the red silk ribbon out of his pocket and tied her hair. She quivered again as he laid a kiss on the back of her neck.

"Red really does suit you," he said.

She ripped her gaze away from his. "I...I need to go."

"You should eat first." He lifted a strawberry out of the basket. At the sight of the tempting dark red flesh, she had to restrain herself from licking her lips.

Before she could insist that she needed to leave immediately, he placed the strawberry inside her mouth. She could not stop herself from sinking her teeth into the fruit. Her taste-buds danced with delight as sweet juices fell onto her tongue.

"Want another?" he asked.

Without thinking, she nodded, her common sense completely eradicated by the delicious fruit.

He fed her strawberry after strawberry. Words of refusal were on the tip of her tongue, but she couldn't bring herself to say them. And they still remained on her tongue when he dropped a chocolate truffle into her mouth. She almost groaned. The truffle had to be one of the best things she ever tasted.

Making her gasp, he put his mouth on hers, licking the chocolate off her lips.

"Chocolate tastes sweeter on you," he murmured.

When he touched the hem of her habit, panic struck her. Was he planning to undress her in broad daylight? Grabbing her basket and forgetting all about her wimple, she jumped up from his lap and ran back to the convent.

Running into the arms of the duke

Persephone was breathless when she arrived at the convent. The sight of the gray stone building brought her relief until she touched her bare head. She cursed under her breath; she'd left her wimple with Thomas.

"Persephone!"

She looked up to see Mary. "What happened to your wimple?" her friend asked, raising her eyebrows.

"Um..." Persephone wanted to curse when she felt her face redden.

Mary teased, "Did you misplace your wimple because you were doing improper things with a man?" When the red in Persephone's face deepened, Mary exclaimed, "You were doing improper things with a man!"

Persephone hissed, "May you please keep your voice down?"

Mary lowered her voice to a dramatic whisper as she continued, "You naughty girl. However, I must admit that I'm somewhat pleased. I adore you, my Persephone, but I always thought that you were too prudish for your own good."

At the words "my Persephone," her heart raced in her chest. Really, why did Mary's use of that possessive pronoun fill her with so much pleasure? And why did Mary's declaration of adoration cause a little pain to strike her heart? Was it because Mary adored her as a friend and nothing more?

Shaking the confusing thoughts out of her head, Persephone said, "If you give me a wimple before Sister Grace sees me, I'll give you these strawberries and chocolate truffles." Persephone had already lost three wimples this year. It was a good thing that the nuns at St. Camilla's

Convent did not believe in corporal punishment, for if they did, Persephone's backside most certainly would've suffered under the thrashing of a cane.

Mary gasped when she saw the contents of Persephone's basket. "Sister Grace let you buy strawberries and chocolate truffles?"

"Well, um, not quite…"

Mary smiled and took Persephone's arm. "I believe you have many things to tell me. By the way, I'm your friend. You don't need to bribe me with sweets to have me help you, but I'll accept the bribe anyway."

For some reason, Persephone felt an ache in her chest at the words, *I'm your friend.* She valued — no, *treasured* — her friendship with Mary, but sometimes, she imagined their friendship blossoming into something else. Sometimes, she longed for it. And always, something in her heart tightened when Mary ran off to meet a boy.

Once they were in Mary's room, her friend closed the door and said, "Tell me everything, Persephone." She reached into the basket and grabbed a chocolate truffle. When she bit into the candy, she moaned. "Oh, this is divine! Did your lover give you these?"

"I do not have a lover," Persephone said, feeling as if her cheeks were on fire.

"But a man did give you these?"

Persephone sighed. "Yes. An arrogant man who I hope to not see again."

"Did he kiss you?"

When Persephone couldn't meet Mary's gaze and touched the lips that Thomas had licked, her friend clapped her hands excitedly. "He did kiss you! Did you like it?"

"It doesn't matter whether or not I enjoyed his kiss. I didn't enjoy his personality."

"My Persephone, it's not like you have to make this man your husband. If you enjoy his kisses, why not have some fun?"

Persephone's pulse quickened as she remembered the duke and Thomas Ellison touching her. Both powerful, wealthy men. Both extremely attractive men. And both men that could be dangerous for a poor noblewoman like her. She shook her head. "I can't see them again."

"*Them?*"

Persephone cursed her mouth.

Mary hissed, "You've been kissing men, *plural*?"

"They kissed me," Persephone said.

"All this time, I thought you were like the Virgin Mary." Mary grinned. "But it turns out you have more in common with Mary Magdalene."

"Oh, you're incorrigible."

"Says the wanton woman who has been meeting strange men, *plural*," Mary teased.

Fiercely, Persephone said, "I don't care about the men! They're not..." She stopped, looking at Mary. Her friend was so beautiful. How could her father claim that redheads were hideous when a gorgeous creature like Mary existed? She wanted to touch that brilliant red hair.

So she did.

She wanted to touch Mary's fair hand.

So she did.

She wanted to touch Mary's plump lips.

So she *almost* did.

Mary placed a gentle but firm hand on Persephone's shoulder when Persephone's lips were mere centimeters away from hers. "Persephone," Mary whispered. "I care about you. I *adore* you. But not like that."

Persephone felt like she could die from mortification. She was such an idiot. Why did she think that Mary would want to kiss her? Why did she think that Mary could be abnormal like her?

"I'm sorry," Persephone mumbled. "I...I..."

Unable to face Mary, Persephone ran out of the room.

"Persephone, wait!"

Despite Mary's shouts, Persephone didn't stop running. She didn't stop running when she was out of the convent. She didn't stop running when she was in the woods. She didn't stop running when an ornate coach appeared.

When Marcus Elham, the Duke of Charlotteshire, looked out the window of his coach and saw the beautiful nun from St. Camilla's Convent, he ordered his driver to stop. The second the carriage stilled, he jumped out and chased after the fair nun.

Persephone caught her breath when she felt an arm wrap around her waist.

"We meet again, fair maiden," the duke breathed into her ear.

At first, she wanted to push him away, but then she thought of Mary. *I care about you. I adore you. But not like that.*

How could such kind words hurt so much?

And how could she return to the convent and ever face Mary again?

She couldn't. She just couldn't.

So she impulsively said to the arrogant nobleman, "Take me away from here."

The best cure for heartbreak is to make out with a hot duke

Marcus blinked, then touched the back of the fair nun's head. "Did your head get injured?" he asked.

"My head didn't get injured. Why, are you accustomed to only concussed women wanting to go anywhere with you?"

His lips twitched. "No, believe it or not, many have called me the master of seduction."

She rolled her eyes. "Does this 'many' consist of the voices in your head?" she muttered.

Slowly, he traced a pattern on the smooth perfection of her pale throat. She shivered. He wanted to show her his mastery of seduction right then and there, but he ignored his aching cock and said, "I'm only inquiring about a head injury because the last time we saw each other, you kicked my shin. Quite hard, in fact."

She bit her lip. Concern filled him when her violet eyes shone with tears. "I just...I just can't return to the convent."

He knit his brow. "Did one of the nuns hurt you?" He'd heard cases of nuns abusing their authority at other convents, of self-proclaimed servants of God refusing to show the mercy of Christ. To his surprise, hot rage burned through his veins at the idea of someone abusing the woman in his arms. If a nun had harmed her, he would do everything in his (very considerable) power to shut down St. Camilla's Convent.

She shook her head. "No, I confessed my feelings to someone, and well...my feelings remain unrequited."

To his further surprise, hot jealousy joined the rage pumping through his veins. He was tempted to kill the man who had stolen and broken her heart, and couldn't help voicing this temptation out loud: "I want to kill him."

She widened her eyes, startled. "Why are you getting so angry? Honestly, even I have no right to be angry. She was so kind..." She widened her eyes even more. "Oh, I shouldn't have said that, especially to you."

She was so kind... So the fair nun was Sapphic? Admittedly, that would be a balm to his ego if that was the explanation for her apparent dislike for him. The jealousy remained, but a little lust mixed with the envy at the image of her making love to another woman. "So...you're an admirer of Sappho's poetry?"

Her fair cheeks turned pink. "Are you going to report my unnatural ways to the church if I answer yes?"

He caressed her throat again. She shivered again and not out of disgust. Could she be like him? "Your secret is safe with me. Besides, far be it from me to call appreciation of the fairer sex a crime." He smiled. "Though I must admit I've experienced the pleasures of my own sex as well."

Her jaw fell. "Oh, do you mean...?"

"Yes." He touched her cheek. "So please do not worry about me exposing you."

She softened. "Thank you for your assurance."

"However, I must ask, are you only interested in women that way or...?"

She scowled. "I'm not interested in you if that's what you're asking. And my disinterest is because of your arrogance, not because of your sex."

"But you asked me to take you away from here."

"Those were impulsive words of folly!"

"I doubt you would've said those words to a man you didn't find attractive..."

"Never mind, I'm returning to the convent — "

His hold on her tightened. "Are you ready to face the woman who broke your heart?" He was aware he was being a manipulative bastard, but he didn't want to let her go.

Her body stilled.

His lips brushed against her throat. "I can help you forget your heartbreak..." He cupped her breast, causing a soft moan to leave her lips.

"Are you seriously seducing a heartbroken maiden?" she hissed. "You truly have no scruples."

"I'm a duke. I have no need for them. By the way, I'm Marcus Elham, the Duke of Charlotteshire."

She glared at him. "I know who you are."

He tilted his head. "You knew I was a duke, yet you didn't immediately swoon into my embrace?"

She snorted. "Believe it or not, yes."

"What's your name?"

With obvious reluctance, she answered, "Persephone."

The corners of his mouth curved up. "May you give me your last name as well?"

With even more reluctance, she added, "Danbury."

The name sounded vaguely familiar. "Is your father a viscount?" Viscount Danbury, despite inheriting a well-managed and profitable estate from his father, was rumored to be nearly destitute due to his fondness for casinos and brothels.

She exhaled. "Yes, unfortunately."

"Do you not care for your father?"

"Why should I care for him if he does not care for me? Do you think I asked him to send me to the convent?"

At the melancholy in her violet gaze, he felt a strange little ache. Without hesitating, he scooped her up into his arms.

"What are you doing?" she asked.

"Fulfilling your request of taking you away from here."

Persephone opened her mouth, about to protest. Then she thought of Mary.

So she closed her mouth and allowed the duke to put her in his coach.

However, she immediately regretted her decision when he pulled her onto his lap and she felt his hardness underneath her. She attempted to kick his shin, but he grabbed her foot before she could give him another bruise.

"Are you scared of me?" he asked. "I'm not going to hurt you."

"I know how you noblemen like to have your way with women." She knew that, yet she allowed the duke to put her in his carriage. What an utter fool she was.

"I'm not going to put your maidenhood in danger." A grin appeared on his handsome face. "Unless you want me to deprive it of safety."

She shot daggers at him. "I'll like my virginity to remain unendangered, thank you very much." She did not find the act of sex to be immoral, but she wanted to avoid its possible consequences. She'd heard one too many stories of pregnant women being abandoned by the men who were responsible for their condition.

He clicked his tongue. "Pity." He lifted her skirts, baring her leg and making her flush. "Are you opposed to me doing other things, however?" He massaged her thigh, causing her to turn warm with pleasure.

She should've hissed, *Yes, I am very much opposed.* Instead, she moaned as he ground his hardness against her, creating a delicious friction that filled the entirety of her body with hot arousal. Then he ripped open the front of her habit. She gasped, then said, "How dare you!"

"I'll dress you in finer clothes later."

Embarrassment warmed her cheeks when he stared at her naked breasts hungrily. Before she could cover herself up, he kneaded her chest. The embarrassment went away and was replaced with bliss. She groaned as her nipple stiffened under his caress. When he closed his mouth over the stiff tip of her breast, her bliss intensified, and her screams filled the carriage.

"Are you all right, miss?" the driver asked in alarm.

"She's all right," the duke answered. "Much more than all right." He licked her nipple, eliciting a moan from her.

"Oh," the driver said. "*Oh*. Well, um, I'll let you know when we arrive at your home, your grace."

"We're going to your home?" Persephone asked.

"Where else would I take you?"

Proper ladies did not visit gentlemen's houses unchaperoned. Then again, proper ladies also didn't get into coaches with handsome men they barely knew, and proper ladies definitely did not attempt to kiss other ladies.

A groan left her throat when the duke cupped her feminine flesh. She was beginning to understand why Mary often ran off to meet young men. If they could make her feel this good, it was a wonder that she didn't run off to meet a young man every night.

Persephone's heart twisted into a knot. She knew that she would never be able to make Mary feel like this. Just as fresh tears threatened to sting her eyes, the duke crushed his mouth to hers, and she was swept up in his kiss.

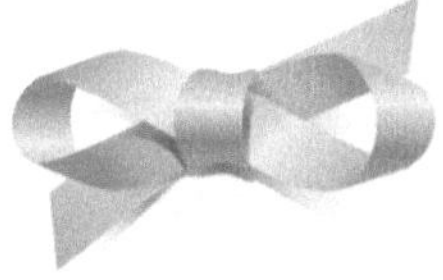

In the duke's bed

By the time they arrived at the duke's estate, Persephone's habit was torn in several places, and Marcus's love bites had marked a few of her body parts. As she crossed her arms over her exposed chest, she said under her breath, "You're an animal."

He murmured, stroking the bud between her legs, "Did you not enjoy my animalistic side?"

She quivered, wishing she could tell him, *I loathed it,* but that would be a blatant untruth.

When he carried her out of the carriage, she was surprised to see that night had already arrived. *Time passes quickly when you're engaging in improper acts with a duke*, she thought.

She was less surprised to see how large Marcus's estate was. Several families could live comfortably in the picturesque house in front of her. The sight of the imposing place would have filled her vain father with envy.

"Your grace, do you require...?" The duke's driver stopped when he noticed Persephone.

She froze, recognizing James, the boy who Mary had met with on the night they'd gone swimming.

Marcus's jaw tightened. "Do you two know each other?" he asked.

James cleared his throat. "Yes, your grace. I'm, um, acquainted with her friend."

The duke relaxed. She furrowed her brow. Would he have thrown a fit of jealousy if James had been "um, acquainted" with her? Why would he think he possessed the right to be jealous? And why did the possibility thrill her a little?

"Oh," Marcus said. "Well, I hope I can count on your discretion, James."

James bowed. "Of course, your grace."

Persephone's stomach twisted into an anxious knot. Despite James's answer to the duke, she worried that James might say to Mary, *You'd never guess where I saw your friend...*

Before she worried herself any further, Marcus went into the house and took her up the grand staircase.

"Are you hungry?" he asked.

Her stomach growled before she could answer with her mouth.

"I'll have one of the maids prepare a tray for us," he said.

She wanted to jump out of his arms and run away when he entered a bedroom. "I told you, I don't want to —"

"I'm not going to steal your innocence," he said, laying her on the big bed.

When she felt the soft silk sheets, she almost let out a groan of pleasure. It had been such a long time since she lay in a luxurious bed like this. All of a sudden, exhaustion came over her. Between getting her heart broken, traveling for hours, and enduring/enjoying the duke's advances, she was in much need of rest.

Her eyes threatened to leave their sockets when the duke began pulling at the sleeves of her habit. "What are you doing?" she asked.

"Undressing you," he said in a matter of fact fashion. "You can't sleep in a damaged habit."

"Whose fault it is for damaging it?" she grumbled, reddening when he bared her chest and backside.

"There's no reason to blush. I've seen you in the nude before."

She glowered at him, pulling the silk sheets over her body. When he kissed her shoulder and felt her breasts through the silk, her scowl faded.

She forced herself to push his hand away. "I'm hungry," she said.

"I'm hungry too," he murmured.

"I'm hungry for *food*."

"All right, I'll feed you, my fair nun." Catching her off guard, he pulled down the silk sheets and kissed the tip of her breast.

She yanked the sheets from his grasp, flushing as she covered herself back up. She shot daggers at him. In return, he shot her a maddening smile.

Once he left the room, she exhaled. What had possessed her to run away with Marcus? Did heartbreak cause people to go temporarily insane?

If Father could see me now... He would have a heart attack. Although he went to bed with prostitutes every night, he had gotten angry at Persephone whenever she so much as had an unchaperoned kiss. "You must have a spotless reputation if you wish to land a husband," he had hissed. "No man wants a whore for a wife."

And certainly, no man wants a whore without a dowry for a wife, she thought. She had no illusions about the duke. He would never marry her, the penniless daughter of a viscount and now a disgraced nun. He likely saw her as a pretty plaything and nothing more. She paled. Oh God, what would she do once he discarded her? Would Sister Grace let her return to the convent? Or would she be forever banned from its walls for the stains she had brought upon her reputation?

Oh God, what have I done?

"Here is your food," Marcus said as he walked into the room with a silver tray. He lifted his eyebrows. "You must be famished. You're even paler than usual."

I was just thinking about my miserable future. The mouthwatering scents of the food distracted her from her bleak thoughts. She nearly drooled when she saw the tray's contents: roasted quail, potatoes swimming in butter, grapes, and a chocolate tart.

"Will this satisfy your hunger?" he asked, sitting next to her and plucking off a grape.

"Yes," she said. "Thank you."

He brought the grape to her lips. When she bit into it, he put his mouth on hers, tasting the fruit's sweet juices on her tongue. She caught her breath as he stroked the back of her neck. God, the handsome duke was dangerous for a girl's maidenhood.

Pointedly, she stuffed her mouth with potatoes, refusing to give him another opportunity to kiss her.

"What's your favorite color?" he asked as she took a bite of the quail, which was tender and flavorful.

"I don't know...red? Why?"

"I need to buy you some clothes tomorrow," he said. "I should get you some fine red gowns."

"You don't need to get me anything fancy. I'm fine with plain clothes."

"I'd prefer to see you in a beautiful red dress."

She muttered, "If you wish to waste your money, who am I to stop you?"

He tugged at the ribbon on her hair. Heat filled her face as she remembered the man who had given her the red ribbon.

"Why are you blushing?" he asked. "Did someone give you this ribbon?" To her surprise, there was a hint of dangerous jealousy in his voice.

"Why do you need to know?"

She gasped when he pulled the ribbon out of her hair and tore the red silk to pieces.

"What possessed you to do that?" she asked, gaping at him.

He clenched his teeth. "I'll buy you some ribbons tomorrow. I don't want you wearing anything that was given to you by someone else."

She scoffed. "What? Are you going to be the sole provider of my clothing from now on?"

"Yes," he answered seriously. He wrapped his arms around her. "I intend to be the sole provider of your meals and sexual pleasure as well."

"Have you gone mad?"

"Mad for you perhaps."

She felt dizzy. "Do you want me to be your mistress?"

"Well, you can't exactly return to the convent since I compromised you. I have to look after you, don't I?"

She couldn't help saying, "Many of your peers wouldn't think so." Too many noblemen thought nothing of ruining a young woman's reputation, then abandoning her to the harsh judgment of society.

"Well, I differ from my peers in many ways."

To be the mistress of a duke... It would provide her with a comfortable lifestyle. And it was certainly better than the miserable future she'd envisioned earlier.

But a mistress was not a wife. Not that she wished to marry Marcus, but it did bring her a little pain to think of him making another woman his wife.

She faked a yawn. "Oh, I'm tired," she said, which was true. It had been a long day, and she welcomed sleep.

"All right."

She expected him to leave the room, but he remained on the bed. She declared, "Uh, I'm going to sleep."

His lips twitched. "Do you expect me to leave my own bedroom?"

"I'll go to another room then — "

He grabbed her before she could climb out of his bed. "I'm not going to let my mistress sleep alone."

My mistress. His use of a possessive pronoun left her quivering with something not unlike delight.

"I haven't agreed to be your mistress," she pointed out.

"But you will."

She disliked his arrogance. And she especially disliked how his arrogance was wholly justified.

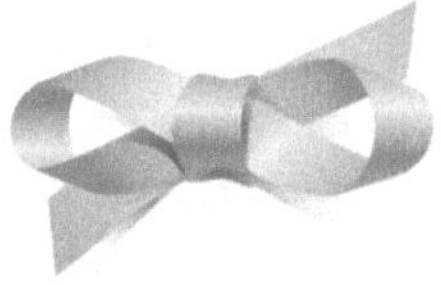

The part in which two friends find out they both want the same woman

The next morning, Marcus groaned as an inconvenient erection started to form in his trousers. It had been a painful exercise in willpower to not ravish Persephone last night. His cock grew more swollen as he thought of her long black curls, deep violet eyes, and plump bosom.

Behind him, his butler entered the room, wishing to ask the duke what he would like for breakfast. However, the butler promptly exited once he saw the bulge in his grace's trousers. The manservant knew better than to disturb Marcus when he was in a state of arousal.

"Whatever has made your cock so hard, friend?"

Marcus jumped at the voice. He glared at his friend Thomas Ellison, who had entered the room unannounced as usual. "What are you doing here?"

"Do I need a reason to visit my dearest friend?" Thomas asked with a smirk, sitting on the sofa opposite Marcus as if he — and not the duke — owned the place.

The staff of life between the duke's legs further hardened at the sight of his friend. When he had told Persephone that he'd experienced the pleasures of his own sex, he had thought of Thomas. His friend and he had never gone beyond the boundaries of friendship, but he'd had midnight dreams featuring Thomas. *Many* dreams. He had wondered more than once what it would be like to put his mouth over his friend's aroused manhood.

"Yesterday, I met a woman," Thomas said. "A beautiful woman."

"What a coincidence. I currently have a beautiful woman in my bed." Marcus had been tempted to kiss Persephone awake, but she had to be exhausted after the events of yesterday, so he'd let her continue sleeping. The second she woke up, he would kick out his friend, politeness be damned.

"She told me her name was Athena, but I believe she gave me a false name. No matter, I'll discover her real identity. I can bribe someone from her convent to give me details about her."

Marcus stiffened. "The woman you met is from a convent?"

"I assume so. She wore a nun's habit." Thomas's eyes turned into slits. "Why?"

"What a coincidence," the duke said again, this time with significantly less humor. "The woman in my bed is from a convent."

"St. Camilla's Convent?"

Marcus's jaw tightened as he nodded. "Violet eyes, fair skin, generous bosom, red ribbon in her black hair?"

Thomas nodded, frowning. "So... it appears that we both desire the same woman."

Hot jealousy ran through the duke's veins. He wanted to both punch his friend's face and suck on his shaft. He wanted to hiss, *She's mine,* and he wanted to hiss, *You're mine.*

"I can see the envy in your eyes," Thomas said with an infuriating smile. "But is your envy directed at me or at her? Or perhaps both?"

Ignoring his friend's questions, Marcus said, "I destroyed your ribbon. And she's already agreed to be my mistress." Technically, she hadn't, but she would eventually agree.

Calmly, Thomas asked, "What if I ask her to be my wife? Marriage offers more security, and you may have noble blood, but I am richer than you."

Marcus tightened his fist. "So are we going to have to duel over her?"

Thomas snorted. "Only idiots participate in duels. Why don't we share her?"

"Share her?"

A corner of his friend's lips curved up. "I know sharing goes against your every instinct as a nobleman, but I'm not willing to surrender her to you." Thomas spread his thighs, displaying his big erection. "Just the thought of her gets me hard like this."

To the duke's shock, Thomas pulled down his pants and let out his swollen manhood. Marcus resisted the urge to lick his lips at the sight of the aroused, hard flesh.

"Thomas, I know you're a commoner, but even you must know it's not proper to reveal your cock in someone's living room," Marcus said dryly. Although Thomas was now incredibly wealthy thanks to his department stores, he was born in a poorhouse. It had taken decades of hard work and a ruthless willingness to cut down his rivals to lift himself out of poverty.

Thomas wrapped his hand around his length. "As if you're not eager to do this too."

Cursing under his breath, Marcus yanked his trousers down, freeing his aching erection. He gripped his staff of life tightly, thoughts of fucking both Persephone and Thomas swirling around in his head.

"Don't you want to lick that gorgeous creature's fair breasts?" Thomas asked, groaning as he squeezed his length. "Don't you want to drink from her cunt like it's the finest bottle of wine in all of England?"

"Yes," Marcus breathed, stroking his rod. God, how he yearned to drink from her cunt and to taste the white seed coming out of his friend's penis.

"Don't you want to sink your cock into her tight little pussy?" Thomas caught his breath, drops of his white seed landing on Marcus's (very expensive) Persian rug.

"You're going to have to buy me a new rug." The duke's own cum fell onto the floor as he imagined filling Persephone's cunt with his manhood.

Thomas didn't answer him. Instead, a cry escaped his throat as he came, covering the Persian rug with more of his white seed.

Marcus came soon after him, cursing as he spilled his cum onto the floor. Good God, how was he going to explain *that* to the servants?

Both of them nearly breathless, the two men stared at each other. The duke swore his friend's eyes were wandering toward his mouth. Did Thomas wish to kiss him? Did Marcus wish that his friend would kiss him?

Thomas cleared his throat. "So are you willing to share her?"

"What makes you think that she would want you?"

With utter confidence, Thomas said, "She will want me if she doesn't already."

Jealousy crept into Marcus at the idea of sharing Persephone with another man. But mixed with the jealousy was a little arousal. The idea of fucking a woman Thomas had sunk his cock into — it was almost like fucking Thomas.

"Fine, if you seduce her, I'd be willing to share her."

Thomas smirked. "'If'? I'm extremely rich and handsome. You mean *when* I seduce her."

Unnoticed by them, the duke's butler entered the room. However, at the sight of their bare cocks and the mess on the floor, the butler immediately left, thinking, *I truly do not get paid enough pounds for this.*

What's better than waking up to a handsome man? Waking up to two handsome men

Persephone woke up to Marcus lying beside her.

"About time you woke up," he said, rubbing her bare shoulder. "It's a quarter past noon."

At the convent, she would've been up by eight o'clock at the latest.

"Hello, *Athena.*"

Her eyes almost jumped out of their sockets. She turned her head and saw Thomas Ellison sitting next to her.

A smirk came onto his lips. "Or should I say, *Hello, Persephone?*"

Was this reality or was she still sleeping? Was this a dream — or a nightmare?

Thomas ran his fingers through her black hair. "I hear my friend destroyed the red ribbon I gave you."

"I refuse to apologize for it," Marcus said.

"You two know each other?" she asked, her heart racing in her chest.

"Yes," Thomas said, pulling her to him.

Marcus scowled, wrapping a possessive arm around her waist. She caught her breath as Marcus lightly bit her shoulder and marked her with a fresh love bite. She turned even more breathless when Thomas marked her other shoulder with a love bite of his own.

She felt like her head was spinning. Just last night, Marcus had offered — well, more like demanded — to make her his mistress. But now Thomas Ellison was touching her as if her body belonged to him. "What is happening?" she breathed, moaning when Thomas kneaded her breasts through the silk bedsheets.

"How would you like to have two men?" Thomas caressed her feminine flesh. She cried out, the silk feeling divine on her sex.

"Two men? You mean, you two would like to share me?" The idea was absolutely mad, but wet arousal formed between her thighs as she imagined the two men both kissing, touching, making love to her.

"I'd prefer to have you to myself," Marcus said, glaring at Thomas. "But my friend says he's unwilling to surrender his claim to you."

"Whoever said that either of you had a claim to me?" she grumbled.

"We'll take care of you," Thomas said. "With us, you'll never want for anything." He lifted the bedsheets from her body. She flushed as both men took in her nudity hungrily.

"How do I know you're not only saying these sweet words to try to seduce me?" she asked. "How do I know you won't just discard me later?"

"We'll never be able to get enough of you, Persephone," Marcus whispered against her throat.

"We'll never let you go," Thomas said, holding her pussy as if he owned her.

Their words were dangerous, seductive, both a promise and a threat.

And foolishly, she desired to give in.

"Okay," she breathed. It wasn't like she could return to the convent, even if she wanted to. And it might have been her naivety talking, but she believed the men when they told her that they would look after her and not abandon her.

Stealing her breath away, Thomas placed his mouth on her feminine flesh. She cried out as his tongue entered her and tasted the most private parts of her.

A combination of envy and desire flooded Marcus when he saw his friend licking Persephone's cunt. Wanting to give her pleasure too, he lowered his head and sucked on her nipple, causing her cries to increase in volume.

The names of both men left Persephone's lips. The sensations were almost too much to take. Almost. But she took them in greedily, gladly.

She arched her back as Thomas thrust his tongue deep into her sex and Marcus licked her stiff nipples.

With a scream, she came.

In the hallway, the maid nearly dropped the tray of food at the sound of Persephone screaming. Worried that the viscount's daughter was in pain, she rushed to the duke's bedroom. However, once she stood under the doorway, she widened her eyes at the wildly scandalous scene. Oh, the viscount's daughter was certainly not feeling pain. The maid hurriedly put the tray on the floor before running to the servants' quarters. Her fellow maids loved gossip, and oh, did she have gossip to serve them!

After Persephone came down from her orgasm, she looked at Marcus. He was staring at Thomas like a man staring at someone he wanted to seduce and not like a man looking at his friend. And Thomas was returning Marcus's gaze with just as much lust in his eyes.

"Are you two...more than friends?" she asked.

"No!" they said too quickly, too loudly.

She glanced at their trousers. They both sported prominent bulges. She said cautiously, "If you two wish to, um, satisfy each other, I wouldn't mind."

Thomas lifted an eyebrow. "What?"

"She knows I've enjoyed the wonders of both sexes," Marcus said.

"You told her that?" Thomas asked in surprise.

She said in a quiet voice, "He told me that after I told him I was, um, rejected by a woman."

Thomas's expression softened. "Oh."

Marcus cupped Thomas's chin. "Then what do you say to letting me help you with the bulge in your trousers, friend?"

"Yes, please," Thomas whispered before groaning as Marcus stroked his erection.

When Marcus pulled Thomas's pants down and held his bare cock, Persephone found herself turning wet again.

Wonder filled Marcus as he squeezed his friend's manhood. He'd dreamed about this so many times, but he'd never imagined that it would ever become reality.

"Harder," Thomas demanded in a low voice.

Marcus obliged, tightening his grip on Thomas's staff of life. Thomas let out a cry, drops of his cum landing on the silk bedsheets. As Marcus ran his hand up and down Thomas's cock, Thomas undid the button on Marcus's trousers. It was Marcus's turn to cry out when Thomas massaged his manhood. Christ, that felt so much better than his own hand.

When Persephone let out a quiet groan, Marcus pulled her to him. As he worked on his friend's cock, he kissed Persephone and rubbed her wet cunt with his other hand. She moaned into his mouth, and by God, he loved consuming her sounds of pleasure.

Just as Thomas spilled his cum into Marcus's hand, Persephone came against his palm, coating his fingers with her feminine arousal.

When Thomas lifted Marcus's sticky hand to his lips and licked the white seed off his fingers, Marcus came with a groan, further ruining the bedsheets.

Two men, one woman, and endless pleasure

"**R**ed truly does suit you," Thomas murmured, holding Persephone's hips.

She looked down at the dress she wore. It was made of fine silk and fit her like a second skin. It'd been such a long time since she'd worn something so luxurious. Then she lifted her head, seeing the various gowns and ribbons that Thomas and Marcus had purchased for her draped all over the sofa. All red, all made of expensive silk.

"You two went overboard," she said.

Marcus kissed her cheek. "You're our woman now. We're obligated to spoil you."

A shiver of delight climbed down her spine. *Our woman* — she very much enjoyed the use of the possessive pronoun.

"I bet you'd look breathtaking in white," Thomas said.

"She would," Marcus agreed.

"You can't be thinking of buying me more clothes," she said. "I already have more than enough."

"But a bride can't wear a red dress," Thomas said.

She squeaked, "Bride? What?"

"I want to make you my wife, Persephone."

Marcus scowled at Thomas. "I want to make you *my* wife."

"You cannot be serious," she said.

"Of course we are," Thomas said. "You belong to us. We might as well make it legal."

She had heard of whirlwind engagements, but this was ridiculous. However, marriage would be practical. Although she was a virgin, she was still as good as ruined. Being the wife of either the duke or Thomas would provide her with security. And she had to admit that the idea of being married to one of them appealed to her.

"If you're my wife, it'll make it extremely difficult for you to run away from us," Marcus said.

She rolled her eyes. Then she said softly, "I have no plans to run away."

"Good." Marcus stroked her face. "You should marry me by the way. My estate is much nicer. Thomas's house is so gaudy."

"But I'm richer, Persephone. And in possession of a bigger cock."

Marcus scoffed, "That may be so, but I'm far more skilled with mine."

She couldn't help laughing at their silly argument. "While I'm flattered that you two are arguing over the honor of taking my hand in marriage, why don't we just draw straws? No matter what, we're all going to be together, right?"

The men both embraced her and kissed the top of her head. "Yes," Marcus said. "No matter what, you're ours and we're yours."

"*Persephone?*"

Her heart raced at the familiar female voice. She turned her head, seeing Mary.

"I've been so worried about you," Mary said.

"Excuse me, who are you and why are you in my living room?" Marcus asked coldly, his hazel eyes slits.

Mary bowed her head ever so slightly, a hint of a frown on her face. "I'm Mary, Persephone's friend from the convent."

Thomas narrowed his eyes. "Are you the woman who broke our Persephone's heart?"

"What?" Mary asked. "Persephone, why — ?"

"Let's speak in private, Mary," Persephone said, trying to ignore the glares Marcus and Thomas directed toward her.

"Absolutely not," Thomas hissed.

An exasperated breath left her lips. "Mary's my friend." A friend that might have broken her heart, but it wasn't Mary's fault that she didn't return Persephone's feelings.

"Fine, we'll allow you 20 minutes," Marcus said.

Mary scoffed. "You cannot be serious?"

Ignoring Mary, Marcus murmured into Persephone's ear, "Remember, you are ours now."

After sending their unexpected guest looks of warning, the men left the room, leaving Persephone alone with Mary.

"I can't believe you ran away from the convent without telling me," Mary said, genuine hurt in her green eyes.

Guilt struck Persephone. "I'm sorry." It had been unfair of her to leave Mary without at least telling her goodbye. Although Mary had rejected Persephone, she was still her dear friend, and she had been kind in her rejection.

"Did I really break your heart?"

Persephone bit her lip, suddenly fascinated with the pattern on the Persian rug. "A little."

"Oh, Persephone." Mary hugged her. "I'm sorry for hurting you."

"You have nothing to be sorry for."

Mary scowled. "Don't you ever again leave without saying goodbye."

"Okay." Persephone said again, "I'm sorry." Then she asked, "How did you manage to get here?"

"James told me that you were here."

So much for James's discretion. But Persephone was glad that James had told Mary.

"You seem to have recovered from your heartbreak pretty quickly," Mary said with a smile. "You managed to land a duke *and* a wealthy tycoon? You're an impressive woman."

A flush came over Persephone's face.

"Which one are you going to marry?" Mary asked. "Are you going to become a duchess? Oh, I would love to brag about being friends with a duchess!"

A smile tugged at Persephone's mouth. "I don't know yet. We might draw straws."

Mary burst into laughter. "That's one of the most absurd things I've ever heard!" She touched Persephone's cheek. "Whoever you decide to marry, please invite me to the wedding."

"Of course."

Thomas and Marcus marched back into the room. The tycoon drew Persephone away from Mary. "Please refrain from touching our woman," he said through gritted teeth.

Mary rolled her eyes. "Friends are allowed to show each other affection, you know."

Unnoticed by Mary, Marcus and Thomas glanced at each other meaningfully.

"And I doubt it has been 20 minutes," Mary pointed out.

"Do you wish to stay for dinner?" Persephone asked, earning scowls from the two men.

"Of course," Mary answered, smirking at Thomas and Marcus. "How can I refuse an invitation to dinner at the house of a duke?"

"Fine, I'll let the cook know we expect another person for dinner," Marcus said. He rubbed Persephone's hip, filling her with heat. "But first, we need to attend to some business."

"Business, right," Mary said dryly. "Well, I suppose I'll find a way to occupy myself before dinner."

"You do that," Marcus said with utter indifference before lifting Persephone up into his arms.

With indecent haste, the duke and the tycoon hurried up the staircase. In Marcus's bedroom, they all fell onto the bed with Persephone lying between the two men.

Marcus slid a hand under her dress and caressed her sex, eliciting moans out of her. "I want to put my cock inside you," he breathed. "But do you wish to wait until the night of the wedding?"

Although she did not think that they would abandon her once they took her virginity, she still said, "I wish to wait." Sex always came with the possibility of pregnancy. She wanted to have the security of marriage if and when she became with child. "If you need to, you can, um, seek satisfaction from other places." It brought her not an insignificant amount of pain to think of Marcus and Thomas going to brothels. But she knew that among high society and the wealthy, it was uncommon for husbands to remain faithful.

Marcus frowned. "I don't wish to sleep with other people."

"And I don't wish to either," Thomas said. "And we certainly don't wish you to 'seek satisfaction from other places.'"

Marcus clutched her feminine flesh possessively. "I don't want anyone in our marriage besides us." Then he said, his lips on her shoulder, "And between Thomas and me, I doubt you'll even have the energy to attempt an affair."

His words left her quivering with arousal. He removed all of her clothing, baring her lovely form. Then he held her close to him, rubbing the bulge in his trousers against her sex. They groaned in unison as her wet heat dripped onto his pants.

Behind her, Thomas left a trail of kisses down her back, causing her skin to tingle. Then he held her breasts. Her moans increased in volume as he caressed her chest until her nipples pebbled underneath his hands. Then seeking relief for his aching cock, he began grinding his erection against her backside.

"Do you like that?" he asked, hoping that her answer would be yes because he desperately didn't want to stop.

"Yes," she said before breaking out in another moan.

Thank Christ, Thomas thought, his hot white seed starting to drip from his cock. He was going to need to change into another pair of trousers after this.

The two men's movements became harder and faster, their cocks demanding release.

"Are you close to coming?" Marcus grunted as her juices started to soak through the fabric of his trousers.

Her answer was a scream of ecstasy. Thomas and Marcus followed her into euphoria, bringing their pants to irrevocable ruin.

Persephone laid her head against Marcus's chest, smiling because she was where she needed and wanted to be.

Epilogue

A *month later*

"You're the most beautiful bride in all of England," Mary said, beaming at Persephone. "Spin around for me one more time."

Persephone rolled her eyes, but she obeyed Mary's command. Despite her assertion that she would've been fine with a simple, inexpensive gown, Marcus had insisted on getting a dress from one of the most sought after modistes in London. She had to admit that the white chiffon dress was absolutely gorgeous and made her look every bit the part of a duchess.

"I can't believe that I'll be able to call myself a very good friend of the duchess," Mary said.

The edges of Persephone's lips curved up. Marcus and Thomas had ended up drawing straws to decide who would become her lawfully wedded husband. Marcus had held up his long straw triumphantly, then had immediately begun bribing/threatening the archbishop into giving him a special license to marry Persephone. After two weeks, he had secured the special license. And a mere two weeks after the acquisition of the license, they were now having their wedding.

Initially, Marcus had planned to have the grandest wedding of the season, but Persephone had persuaded him to have a smaller ceremony at his estate. She had no desire to mingle with all of high society, and she had pointed out, "A smaller wedding means the less you'll have to wait to consummate the marriage."

That had certainly convinced him and Thomas.

"So Thomas is walking you down the aisle?" Mary asked.

"Yes," Persephone said. Predictably, her father had tried to contact her after he'd heard that she was getting married to the duke, but she'd tossed his letters into the trash without looking at them. In her father's absence, Thomas had volunteered to walk with her during the ceremony.

"How unconventional. The bride typically doesn't fornicate with the person who gives her away."

"Mary!" Persephone exclaimed, blushing.

Mary laughed. "How can you still blush so much when you're involved with two men *simultaneously*?" She looked at the clock. "We should go soon. Marcus will throw a fit if we're so much as a moment late. That man is impatient to make you his wife."

• • ❦ • •

MARCUS WAS INDEED IMPATIENT to make Persephone his wife. When he saw her walk down the aisle with Thomas, the sight stole his breath. Persephone looked so beautiful, and Thomas so handsome. He could not wait to consummate the marriage. It took most of his willpower to not demand the priest to hurry up with his goddamn speech. When the duke kissed his bride, it took *all* of his willpower to not make love to her right then and there.

He had endured the reception for approximately five minutes before pulling Persephone toward the staircase.

"Shouldn't we eat dinner with the guests?" she asked.

"I'll tell a maid to bring dinner up to our room later," he said. "I need to have you. *Now*."

"You are the king of dramatics," she said. But he noticed her shiver with thinly-veiled delight.

As soon as they were on the bed, he began taking off her clothes, cursing all of the laces and layers. Why were wedding dresses so damn complicated?

The moment she was naked on the silk bedsheets, Thomas entered the room. "You started without me? How rude."

"Sorry, Marcus is being extremely impatient," Persephone said before gasping as Thomas kissed the underside of her breast. Then he kissed Marcus's chest, causing the duke's cock to swell even more.

Thomas put her on his lap, kneading her bosom. As her nipples stiffened against his fingertips, his cock hardened underneath her. His manhood felt like it was near the point of bursting when Marcus lay before Persephone's cunt. The duke licked his lips before thrusting his tongue into her sex, causing the room to fill with her cries.

Just as Persephone was on the precipice of a climax, Marcus drew her into his arms. He held her feminine flesh. "Are you ready to consummate the marriage?" he asked.

She swallowed, then nodded. Anxiety pumped through her blood but also excitement.

Marcus opened his trousers, freeing his aching erection. As his cock entered her, she caught her breath.

"Does that hurt, wife?" he asked in a gentle voice.

She shook her head. "No." Having his cock inside her felt strange but also good. And when he pushed his cock deeper into her sex, it felt even better.

"I love you, Persephone," Marcus said. "And I love you, Thomas."

Thomas and Persephone gave him matching smiles. "And I love both of you," she said.

"And I love both of you," Thomas said before kissing Persephone and Marcus.

Marcus hissed as her pussy tightened around his staff of life. Bloody hell, that felt amazing. With a groan, he spilled his seed inside her.

"Do you want your turn, Thomas?" she asked.

"Oh, I want my turn," Thomas said in a voice that was thick with desire. "But are you sure you're up for it? I know women can be sore after their first time..."

She embraced him, putting her lips on his. "I'm up for it."

The tycoon then wasted no time taking off his pants, even ripping them in his eagerness. He slid his manhood into her sex, eliciting a cry out of her. She moved her hips toward him, encouraging him to push his staff of life deeper into her cunt.

Her sex gripped his cock. He moaned, loving the sensation.

Then they came together, their moans becoming one.

Thomas looked at Marcus. The duke's cock had again become swollen with lust. Running his tongue over his lips, Thomas leaned over to taste the tip of Marcus's manhood. Marcus cried out, spilling a drop of cum into Thomas's mouth. The tycoon swallowed the delicious drop before closing his mouth over Marcus's erection.

"Oh God!" Marcus shouted as Thomas sucked on his shaft. Thomas couldn't decide which was sweeter — Marcus's seed or Persephone's nectar. Both were things he would wish to taste during his final moments.

Marcus came, filling Thomas's mouth with his cum. Thomas drank him readily, the evidence of the duke's climax almost bringing him to another orgasm.

The two men then held their lovely Persephone, vowing to keep her with them forever and always.

Sign up for my newsletter to get a free book!

Get *In the Dark: An Insta-Love Story* for free if you sign up for my newsletter here[1]. In addition, you'll hear about my new releases and get access to exclusive sales/freebies!

---

1. https://storyoriginapp.com/giveaways/5fbe502e-1570-11eb-a09f-67946e2bdeae

Connect with Me!

Thank you so much for reading! <3 If you enjoyed this story, please consider leaving a review.

If you want to connect with me, you can do so via the following platforms.

Goodreads: https://www.goodreads.com/author/show/17011380.Isla_Chiu

Email: islachiu@gmail.com

Don't miss out!

Visit the website below and you can sign up to receive emails whenever Isla Chiu publishes a new book. There's no charge and no obligation.

https://books2read.com/r/B-A-TNDF-UPOQB

BOOKS 2 READ

Connecting independent readers to independent writers.

Also by Isla Chiu

Alpha Male U
Dare
Safe
Professor

Indecent Proposals
Office Hours: A Student and Professor Story
Loving the Chase
Taken by the Casino Owner

OTT Enterprises
Dear Mr. CEO, I Want You
Dear Mr. CFO, I Hate You
Dear Mr. Counsel, I Need You
Dear Mr. Chairman, I Want to Have Your Baby

Standalone
His Sweet Little Addiction

Just Because of You
A Night with Paradise Four
Taking the Bride
You Equals Mine
Claiming His Runaway Bride
Catching His Thief: A Thanksgiving Insta-Love Story
Kidnapping the Bride
Ringing in the Lunar New Year
The Only One that I Want
The Obsessed Husband
Caught by the Men of the House
Call Me Oppa
Breaking His Rules
Taking Our Bride
Claiming Our Runaway Bride
Sparks Fly: A New Adult Friends to Lovers Romance
Her Cookies: A Student and Teacher Insta-love Story
Quick & Dirty: 3 Stories
Hello, Alpha Male: A Romance 5 Book Bundle
Tempting Him: A Dad's Best Friend Story
His Pretty Prisoner
He Knows What He Wants: A Romance 5 Book Bundle
Her Elegant Prison
Blackmailed by the Jerk
Alpha Male Blast from the Past
Caught in the Act
Compromising the Earl's Daughter
Obsessed with Her: A Romance Collection
Wanting His Student
Claimed on Halloween: A Vampire Romance
His Enchanting Princess
His Lovely Prisoner
My Best Friend Forever

A Werewolf Jock for Thanksgiving
Enchanted by You: A Romance Collection
To Have Her: An Alpha Male Romance Collection
You're Mine, Wife
Her Beautiful Captor: A Captive Romance Collection
His Exquisite Prisoner
My First Theft Went a Little Like This
A Werewolf Jock for the New Year
Taking Back My Bride
So Much More
My Immortal Valentine
Short and Not So Sweet: A Short Story Collection
Caught by Mr. Smith
Bad Habits: A MMF Romance

Watch for more at https://kissmeseriously.wordpress.com/.

www.ingramcontent.com/pod-product-compliance
Lightning Source LLC
Chambersburg PA
CBHW031426160726
47993CB00003B/1416